Twisted Love in Thunder Bay

IMOGENE GRANT

Zeta Publishing, Inc
P.O. Box 953
Silver Springs, FL 34489
www.zetapublishing.com

This is a work of fiction. All of the characters, names, incidents, organizations, and dialogue in this novel are either the products of the author's imagination or are used fictitiously.

The views expressed in this work are solely those of the author and do not necessarily reflect the views of the publisher, and the publisher hereby disclaims any responsibility for them.

Ordering Information:
Quantity sales. Special discounts are available on quantity purchases by corporations, associations, and others. For details, contact the publisher at the address above.
Orders by U.S. trade bookstores and wholesalers. Please contact Zeta Publishing: Tel: (352) 694-2553; Fax: (352) 694-1791 or visit www.zetapublishing.com

ISBN: 978-1-950340-08-8 (sc)
ISBN: 978-1-950340-09-5 (e)

Library of Congress: 2019911159
Printed in the United States of America

EPISODE ONE
1995

THE CORSICAN SYNDROME

DeHaven Manor stood majestically above the carefully manicured grounds, as twilight approaches... Thunder Bay.

On a veranda overlooking a Lagoon with towering waterfalls, CAROLINE DeHaven sat trying to find a comfortable position for her swollen, pregnant belly. Caroline is beautiful in spite of her pregnancy. She watches her husband CARTER DeHaven as he rode up the lane on Sammie his favorite energetic stallion.

Carter is a handsome man, white shirt open at the collar sitting comfortably in the saddle; his riding clothes fit him like an elegant glove.

A man stood in the growing shadows watching, eating sunflower seeds, he moves surreptitiously closer among the shrubbery toward the Veranda and the unsuspecting woman there, when he heard a horse and rider coming closer at a fast clip.

The intruder is handsome in a tough way, a scar from the right eye to his chin after having been in numerous brawls... the scar added to the ruggedness of his face.

Carter stopped in front of the Veranda, saying "Are you alright and where's your nurse I told her not to leave you alone."

Caroline said laughing, "I'm fine dear the nurse had business in the little nurse's room nosey."

Carter amused said, "Since you put it that way, I want to put Sammie away, will you be alright?"

"I'll be alright." She said.

He pressed, saying "Okay if you are sure."

"I'll be here and just fine. "She said.

Sammie made noise in his throat, pawed at the ground.

Caroline continued, saying "Who knew horses could be impatient, go sweetheart put him away. I'll be here when you get back." She repeated, "I never knew a horse could be impatient." laughing playfully... her laugh turns her face from lovely to very pretty.

"See 'ya in a bit..." Carter said as he turned to go, he pointed at her.

"You made your point, I'll stay put, now go and put Sammie away." She said.

"You are a sweetheart... stay put my lovely, I mean it you stay put." Carter stressed.

Carter galloped away to the barn.

Neither saw the shadow of the man lurking secretly among the shrubbery. Carter stopped to talk with his foreman as he turned Sammie's reins over to the groom.

The man materialized jumped easily over the rail to the veranda.

Caroline frightened asked, "Who are you? What do you want...my husband is near?"

The intruder said, "Quiet ...and you want be hurt." As he moved threaten toward her.

Caroline screamed.

The man tries to quiet her and stop the screams... with his hand over her mouth.

She bites his hand and scratched him over a scar on his face... he hurriedly strikes Caroline over her swollen abdomen... and threw her screaming to the floor...she fights back kicking and screaming as much as her condition would allow.

The man after his attack raced quickly away through the lush shrubbery.

Police sirens sounds loudly as they race through the streets... to DeHaven Manor.

Caroline's screams echoed through the hills reaching the barn, the neighbors and the deepest recesses of the Manor, Carter and all the servants converged on his wife as she held her abdomen, watery blood spilled on the floor.

Her screams were heard by neighbors ...several people called the police saying, "Someone on DeHaven Manor is being killed....hurry!"

Police followed enforce, to DeHaven Manor, Detectives, laboratory, finger print men, photographers, and later dogs searching for the scent of the killer.

Police in their search found the sun flower seed shells, in the thugs hiding place under the hedges where he had stood.

Search dogs found and followed the path the culprit had followed and scrambled over the wall.

The assailant had rushed through the shrubbery to the nearest wall and climbed over to the outside and the waiting Lincoln Towne Car… that sped away only allowing the attacker to hurriedly draw his leg inside the automobiles.

Carter rushed to his wife, lifted her to the chase lounge…cradled her in his arms giving orders, saying,"IKE, call Doctor Morton!!! Hurry. Get a move on man! Bessie call the police!"

He looks at his crying wife, saying, "Everything will be alright, I'm here now try and relax sweetheart." He pauses momentarily, and then asked, "Did you see who did this?"

Carter turns to MINNIE he said, "We need towels… lots of towels." Minnie ran for towels,

Carter continues repeats, "Sweetheart did you see who did this?" he cradled her in his arms saying, "Oh my sweetheart Doctor Morton is on his way, I'm here, now."

DR. MORTON rushes into the veranda examines Caroline quickly, saying," Minnie I'll need the two maternity kits, gowns, sterile towels, gloves …"

MINNIE standing nervously from one foot to the other, asked, "Doctor… you mean the birthing kits?"

SECONDS LATER:
Dr. Morton calmly answers, "Yes Minnie get someone to help you, I'll need the incubators, hurry girl… and calm down you have to help me until my nurses get here… now… Minnie I need you to hurry." He turns to the in house nurse said, "Nurse James I need you to start the intravenous drip give me two lines to start, can you do that? Then I need you to assist me after I scrub. I have to perform a classic- emergency c-section."

The nurse nods and started to do as he asked.

Caroline's cries were growing weaker. She said, "The man hit me, it hurts so much."

Carter said, "Dear, sweetheart I want you to hold me tight like you've never done before hold on to me we'll get through this together," then pressed his lips to her forehead.

DR. MORTON a fatherly appearing figure turns to Carter saying, "Carter we don't dare move her now we have to do a Classic- C-section right here, she's in active labor, and you attend to your wife. I'll take care of this…" as he worked feverishly to slow the bleeding.

Dr. Morton saying quietly, "Carter, Caroline is tearing and losing too much blood who ever struck her ruptured the Uterus I need to open the intravenous... damn rotten thing for anyone to do... hit a pregnant woman hard enough to endanger the babies... and hard enough to rupture her uterus... the babies are in mortal danger."

Caroline cried, anxiously, "My babies he hurt my babies!!! Carter, are they alright?"

Carter held her lovingly in his arms answered, saying soothingly, "Don't worry sweetheart Doctor Morton is here taking care of everything... we're getting there." he cradled her head against his chest and looked worried at the doctor as the doctor feverishly did his job.

The children were born, and to the surprise of those in attendance saw the babies were conjoined twins, joined at the scapula and parietal both heads.

MUCH LATER:

What seemed like hours the babies were clean and wrapped with warm blankets and make shift skull caps in their incubator. The smaller of the twins was having difficulty breathing.

Dr. Morton asked? "What are their names?"

Caroline answered, "The stronger is PHILLIP DeHaven his brother PETER DeHaven," her weakened voice almost a whisper, nearing death said, "Carter, please I want to see our babies."

The incubator was taken to her side ...

Nurse JAMES said, "We can't take them out of the incubator, If Mr. DeHaven helps you to sit up slightly to see them."

Carter raised Caroline she smiles at her children then asked, "Which is the stronger?"

Nurse James answered, "The one sucking on his fist."

Caroline smiled, "The little scamp, he'll have to take care of his little brother. Carter, thank you for our lovely family, now sweetheart I think I'll get some rest I've had a busy day."

Carter held her in his arms as his precious Caroline breathed her last breath.

He buried his face in her hair in remorse sobbing her name, "Caroline, why did he have to take you from us?" saying over and over. "Caroline, Caroline my darling Caroline, my wife, my lover ... mother of our babies why did it have to be you!!!??? Oh Lord Why, why her?"

Doctor Morton in sorrow helped him up so the servants could dress her.

A large crew of police spent hours as they searched through the trees and shrubs, all the grounds they found footprints, a strip of fabric that tore when the assassin climbed the wall, the man had scraped his skin left tiny bits of flesh with a smear of blood, the samples were very carefully collected.

Police canvassed the neighborhood asking about the automobile that had waited under the shadow of the trees along with the men in it.

At the break of dawn the police crew had packed and gone, only the detectives stayed to talk with the servants, the doctor and Carter.

Detectives SWARTZ decided to talk with Carter whose wife had delivered twins and died from the killer's brutal attack.

LIBRARY DeHaven Manor:

Detectives found Dr. Morton with Carter pacing the room in his grief and over powering anger.

The lead Detective said, "I am Detective SWARTZ, and my partner Detective SHAW... we are so sorry for your loss...but we have a few questions to ask if we may."

Doctor Morton said, "We will help all we can...ask your questions."

Detective Swartz asked, "Is there anything you can tell us?"

Detective Shaw added, "No matter how small would help us find the killer."

Carter answered saying, "My wife said before she died... the man had a scar on one side of his face... from his right eye to his chin."

Dr. Morton added. "Caroline scratched him in the face... I don't know if her kicks were effective, but she did kick him..."

"He was white...a big man... leaped the rail to the veranda...so he was possibly athletic." Carter said, he paused momentarily added vehemently, "Cowardly son of a bitch... he had to see Caroline was pregnant ...he could have killed my boys, too," ...a catch in his throat....as he was overwhelmed with grief.

Detective Swartz said, "We will not ask any more questions... We just had a call ...there is a chase with a Lincoln Towne Car... the chase is on along the great highway now...."

Detective Shaw, "...Again... We are sorry for your loss we will head for the chase...we'll let our self out."

At the wreck of the Town Car...one occupant was thrown clear... his body a tangled mass of dead humanity....the scar was evident in his mangled face... the area was cleared of the wreckage.

DAYS LATER:

Carter Said, "Doctor Morton I have to protect my boys can you help me?"

DR. Morton answered, "You and I talked about your problems, with

SELLERS Conglomerate trying a takeover of DeHaven Enterprises, I'm working on that for you now, I've taken the boys up to EAGLES LAIRE, I have a clinic there where DR. JEFFERY SLAUGHTER and I will do the surgery to separate the twins as soon as PETERS respiration problems are resolved it's not a big problem really, they'll have to be separated... might as well do the circumcision as well."

Dr. Morton paused momentarily, in deep thought then said

"My sister -in-law ABIGAIL SUMMNER will take PHILLIP, I will take PETER. I'm retiring, my wife and I are going to travel and later settle in Europe... the twins will be separated and safe until they can control their lives, and know why they might have to defend themselves."

Carter said, "I've taken care of them financially, DeHaven Manor will never be sold out of the DeHaven family... You or I will be around when the time comes for them to know why they were separated...keep a running account of what happened. That is if I am not here to tell them... they will never have to need for anything."

"We have noticed a peculiar thing about the boys. If one has discomfort the other feels it and cry or make a noise my nurse noticed and we have kept notes on the causes... everything... it's the Corsican Syndrome, as I've read, it makes a closer bond than regular identical twins... although it happens in identical twins at times."

DETECTIVES were shown in, one said, "I am Detective MARTIN SWARTZ, this is my partner ALAN SHAW..."

They acknowledged the police.

Det. Shaw said, "I am sorry to intrude in you grief again but we would like to ask a few more questions about the attack on your wife... could it have been you he was after?"

Carter answered, "We haven't a clue officer, when the assassin struck... why Caroline and she was pregnant he came out of spite, jealousy or whatever the hell he had in his mind we have no idea." He was silent momentarily, said, "It could have been a message to me... I have problems with Sellers Conglomerate but would they go so far as to murder my pregnant wife, she was so helpless, what kind of cold blooded animal could murder like that who could do such a thing."

Swartz responded."We are working on it sir, the passenger in the car. he ate sun flower seeds in wait, we found shells spilled from the automobile as it went over the cliff, the killer burned to death when the car went over the cliff... the heavy Towne Car burned so hot nothing was left of the remains even his teeth crumbled...there had to be an accelerant for it to burn so hot."

Carter said, "We can't think of a reason they chose to murder my wife...he could see she was pregnant and couldn't defend herself, a cowardly act if it were me he was after I was at the barn in plain sight...

that's taking greed and hatred to far... why not me? I don't understand ...I am sorry, I can't talk about it, the memory is too fresh now, with my Caroline lying with my sons in her casket." He turned away his grief was overwhelming to observe.

The Detectives made their apologies and departed.

FAMILY MAUSELEUM:
Caroline's memorial with open casket, she was displayed with babies corpses, on either side of her.

Carter was devastated; he sat beside the casket long past the ceremony, he and the mourners slowly moved away after his family was safely sealed inside their resting place.

A lone man unnoticed perched in the shadows of the trees high on a hill with a long distance snipers rifle, and binoculars observing the attendance at the memorial service.

Carter and those who attended the memorial were slowly making their way toward DeHaven Manor...when snipers bullets peppered the side of the mausoleum wall: screaming, the mourners scatters for cover... two were struck and collapses with superficial leg wounds.

Dr. Morton treated their wounds... using make shift tourniquets with, ties and handkerchiefs'...guards on duty went into action...stormed the hill to find the sniper had gotten away without leaving an indication of anyone had been lying in wait.

Police searched the area thoroughly but to no avail.

EAGLES LAIRE
Carter DeHaven stood watching his sons sleep, safe from the dangers of his enemies.

HOURS LATER:
K.I.S.G., STUDIOS UP TO THE MINUTE NEWS
The newscaster reported saying excitedly, "This just in Ladies and Gentlemen...Carter DeHaven, was gun down tonight on his estate. The bullet entered his heart killing him instantly... outside his home ladies and gentlemen in, Palmetto Springs...no witnesses. His wife was murdered months ago, she was pregnant with twins that died with the mother... weeks later the night guard stopped a break in of the mausoleum when a grave robber seemingly set on robbery of the corpses... only the babies bodies were disturbed."

MONTHS PASS:
POLICE HEADQUARTERS
Detective Swartz ...saying to their supervisor, "Our squad has been

cut...we are just spinning our wheels on this DeHaven case and getting nowhere fast... The servants were accounted for...There was the break in to the mausoleum and Mrs. DeHaven crypt... and the sniper fire at the memorial service...we found nothing...the shooter was a professional... there is big money behind it all."

Shaw added, "The bullet that killed DeHaven could have been bought anywhere, the gun was a twenty two rifle that used 22 long ammunition all very common, can be found in gun shops in that kind of neighborhoods. The guy was a professional a crack shot, he probably could have killed DeHaven from two blocks away."

"I told the chief we did our best for the poor guys suffering. SELLERS CONGLOMERATE all had alibis and were someplace else, and you know they were lying, the decision was made before the murders, no one can prove it, damn convenient, a car belonging to them was reported stolen and found at the bottom of KARL'S canyon completely destroyed, one body was burned beyond recognition... the other found, to show the scar." Swartz said as leaving the office. Then said, "After the job we had to do on the guys little family I felt bad having to hit his pregnant wife."

"That's water under the bridge, old news. Get over it." his partner said.

"Hey not so loud... let's get out of here loud mouth... the boss was lucky we were on hand to investigate the case...he is sure they would go nowhere."Shaw said.

Aunt Abigail's bedroom years later as she took her last breath in death.

Aunt Abigail's funeral service, Phillip stood at the graveside:
FLASHBACKS crowded his mind remembering Aunt Abigail, had a fear of germs... the hot baths, hand washing, dressing Phillip in pastel colors. Long hair she always addressed him as her angel Phillipa.

The fights he had in private school when kids who said "look at the 'little girl' by jeering school children.

Phillip beat the kid to within inches of his life.

Abigail would not allow him to see a special girl, actually she forbade him to see or mention her name.

He was removed from private school... to the many Private Tutors began, and the long travels to other countries. Her last words to Phillip "In spite of everything I have loved you and wanted to keep you safe. I insisted that you learn the businesses and you are one of the best. After my burial, see your Uncle Morty he has everything you'll need." She closed her eyes said, "I have to rest now."

Abigail died later in the night.

TWENTY TWO YEARS HAS GONE BY:
2017
DR. MORTONS HOME OFFICE NIGHT

An older Dr. MORTON stood to welcome PHILLIP DeHaven the first arrival. The young man was dressed elegantly in a pale gray suit with coordinating accessories.

MOMENTS LATER:

Dr. Morton said, "I have someone I want you to meet, and here he is right on time, Peter DeHaven, meet your brother Phillip DeHaven your twin."

PETER DeHaven entered a more laid back handsome athletic young man. Phillip stood, both men stopped in shock as they recognized the other man before them was an exact look alike.

Phillip was the first to recover said, "I've always felt there was more to my life than the one I have lived." he turned to Dr. Morton with a questioning look.

Peter is still in awe of the exact look alike who sounded like him, he walked around his new found brother completely in awe.

Dr. Morton said, "I brought you here to tell you what you have to face."

Phillip asked "Why now Uncle Monty? Aunt Abby never said."

"Your mother Caroline and your dad Carter DeHaven were murdered.

Caroline was pregnant with you. Conjoined twins Dr. Slaughter and I performed the surgery to separate you.

Dr. Slaughter has died, Abby had a heart attack is dead.

Weeks later after the surgery Carter was gun down in his drive way…. We had to separate you again physically and send you out of harm's way… Now you are grown up and can be at each other's back."

Peter said, "That explains the scar on my back and the patch of hair being a different color."

Dr. Morton answered saying, "I bought you here because Abigail has died, my wife had a heart attack we are getting older, you have to know about your parents and how they died, and you had to be protected in the mean time until you could protect yourself."

Peter asked, "How did they die I never could get a straight answer?"

Dr. Morton answered, "Your mother was bludgeoned on her pregnant abdomen which called for your surgery. Caroline died that night and Carter was gunned down weeks later. That brings us to why you had to be separated. Your father was being forced not in a pleasant way to sell his property … threats, live stock and other animals were poisoned some dirty things were done especially to force a way to force sale of DeHaven Enterprises, Carters planed it so they could never buy the business and

DeHaven Manor."

Phillip asked, "Why us and why now... how do we know they didn't give up after twenty years?"

Dr. Morton answered... "There was a break in at the DeHaven mausoleum, Caroline's cubicle was vandalized ...Dr. Slaughter used forethought and had added two infant corpses to her coffin, sure enough the dead babies bodies had been disturbed... our conclusion the killers did not want any DeHaven's alive from that family branch...Be careful you could be in danger even now... DeHaven Manor has been watched throughout your life time. We know its SELLERS Conglomerate... our problem is we can't prove it... they cover their tracks, and lots of money has been poured into getting DEHaven property."

"I heard that...people were saying Abigail was the nut of the times." Phillip said.

Peter replied, "Crazy she was not...when you think of what she has done for us."

Dr. Morton continues."Abigail formed a women's group and built a compound in the trees for little people to keep surveillance for us. There has been strange happening on the Sellers estate especially at nights... strange lights, increased guards...all kinds of skullduggery."

The women IDA, MARTHA and BERTHA were members or rather they were instructors of special Ops in service. Abby built them a home on the bluff in the trees ...they along with the little people have a home for life there."

Peter asked, "Have you found anything concrete... solid information we can use in a court of law?'

Phillip asked, "This is why you gave us these folders?"

Dr. Morton "That's the best way for me to keep you up to date on your heritage and the dangers you might face when we brought you home, all the players are in your folders we followed them through the years, most are still alive those that died we crossed off, folders are accurate.... Up to date"

Peter acknowledged, "We appreciate your thoughtfulness we'll be cautious, thanks. Do you have an idea what they could be doing On Sellers grounds?"

Dr, Morton answered, "They have armed guards, we haven't been able to go near the place. It's one reason Abigail formed the women's group...they will be here tonight...the little people are sharp shooters, have the ability to read lips, sharp shooter from their youth, and other things...you'll meet them later."

Phillip said. "I will be glad to see IDA again; she's a crack up... You'll like them Peter ...they kept me safe for twenty years."

Dr. Morton said, "...as I was about to say... they all were in special ops, as instructors... and did their service for our country..."

Peter asked, "What about the little people?"

"Yes, Abigail built their house on the bluff among the trees ...really nice." He continues. "Oh I'm forgetting the colony for the little people in the trees.... In the colony are very artful with their arts and crafts projects. ...The people from far and near... shops there...Abigail liked them especially... she built the compound of little people... A tough bunch, their families were born in the circus, sharp shooters and other expertise."

Phillip chuckled, "You know brother, forewarned now we know everything, and we have to talk. I had dreams about you; I mean waking dreams you invaded my thoughts at the dimmest times. "He paused momentarily, then said as the door opens, in comes three women ... Phillip went to them saying..."Peter here is the three women I adore... This is IDA, BERTHA and MARTHA they kept me safe even though they dressed me like a girl." All laughed.

Ida asked "Did you tell them about my innate cussedness... and my mean streak? " She said with a straight face... In a pleasant tone of voice.

MARTHA added, "That ain't the half of it...wait till you get to know her...she can piss you off, too."

BERTHA laughing said."You're being too hard on her...tell the real truth."

Ida said, "My audience...what I have to put up with everyday... are we done? I'm really known as wonderful."

Phillip replied, "Not yet Doc. was just explaining about twins born joined together."

Dr. Morton said, "About that, it's a phenomenon that has been written about, conjoined twins can know when one twin is in trouble the other feels the trouble and even the pleasures of each other, and some identical twins has a premonition also."

Phillip said, "Glad you're in our corner Uncle Morty. "

Doctor Morton added, "Oh I added a new packet of information... Your Aunt Abigail investigated the area she found... caves, we need to look them over. One reason there are caverns for illegal storage we can look at them later...my wife is waiting I have to go now for real." He started to leave, saying "I didn't add to your pack...Abby thought there was a master mind behind Biggars...we could never find... several tried to follow him in the helicopter... always lost him in the hills."

Phillip asked, "Could it have been just a pleasure flight to clear his mind...to clear his thoughts?"

"I don't think so...he always had fresh ideas after those flights...Biggars is great at organization with his teams... I can't explain it... the plans were more refined and to the point."Dr. Morton said at a loss for words.

"The man I read about in my notes...his yelling and posturing, talking to his dog is a controlling technique just to control the troops...not crazy... and there could be a master mind in the background."Peter said.

Dr. Morton said," I really have to go my wife is waiting...probably mad as hell."

Ida said..."We'll go with you ..." To her friends, "Come on you snitches... they should get to know me gradually....you can't just spring it on them suddenly." they left the room laughing and talking.

Dr. Morton stood and said, "Stay here and talk all you want in your packets you will find my fortune, I have given you both to take that adversary on, I kept enough for me and my wife quite enough for retirement, now have your talk I'll see you later," after thought Doctor Morton said,"Oh, if you haven't noticed the one difference in you, Phillips eyes are green Peters are blue, your parents eyes, mothers blue Carters green. I'd better hurry my wife is having a bad night..." he turned and left the room.

The young men turned to look at each other Peter said, "Could we talk later at my apartment? I have someone waiting for me, and here she is."

The shapely young woman stood in the doorway saying, "There you are, I am late and hungry." Her voice was husky and low, a tall shapely figure the envy of any runway model, well turned long legs shown in her tennis outfit, her coffee and cream complexion glowed in the light... her walk as she crossed the room was sensual.

Peter continued from the shadows, "Here she is now KASSI KNIGHT, love of my life."

Phillip stood and turned as Kassi crossed to the wrong twin and kissed him soundly on the lips.

Peter said, "Kassi, sweetheart you kissed the wrong one."

She leaned back looking at Phillip embarrassed, stepped back apologizing profusely. Went to Peter and said, "I'm so sorry, wait a minute, you are twins!!! You didn't tell me you were a twin!" she exclaimed looked from one to the other in awe and disbelief.

Peter answered laughing, "Join my club I didn't know until today, meet my brother Phillip DeHaven my twin brother."

Phillip smiling, "The pleasure is mine to meet such an outgoing affectionate, young woman. Peter we must 'all' stay in touch."

Kassi said, "I am pleased to meet you Phillip but I have to go, I have rehearsal in an hour."

Peter added, "Kassi is a marvelous singer, that's how I met her she has been singing to me ever since. Come on baby I'll take you to rehearsal... Phillip we have to meet later tonight at the Manor, is that okay?"

Phillip answered, "Ten's alright?"

Peter nods, as he and Kassi walked arms around each other, Kassi's slim waist, one noticed her flaring hips as her sensual swaying body crossed to the door.

She spoke softly, "Can we get some food, and I am starved."

Peter amused, "I have to drive you and feed you, too, wow? You're tough, but cute."

"Why not, I waited for you sir." She said hugging him around his middle as they left the room.

Peter said, "If I must, I will, bring your little sexy self on."

Kassi asked, "Did I ever tell you…when my parents died …I inherited a light house on the San Francisco Peninsula…my dad liked light houses?"

"No … you have so many sides…" Peter said.

"WE have to go there sometime; it's a blast for relaxing." She replied.

Phillip watched the exchange with envy.

Morning in the Carter family mausoleum, Phillip and Peter stood beside the crypts of Carter and wife Caroline DeHaven's burial sites, in the family mausoleum… their parents life sized photographs stood between their resting sites.

PHILLIP said "You realize someone has robbed us of a lifetime with our parents… they were a great looking couple."

"Yes and we can't let them get away with that. I am for finding the killers who ordered that catastrophe…we have friends to recruit…kids, sons and daughters plus other relatives… we need eyes and ears , those who know people that will contact people in high places." he paused, then said, "I'll meet you at the manor this evening I need to contact some of my ole buddies. I will explain to them." Peter answered.

Phillip caught up in the moment saying ,"I'll contact my ladies who kept me safe for twenty years they taught Special Ops in service to the country…and some of my friends that are ready for a fight…we'll get this show on the road." They hug… then went on their mission.

THE NEXT MORNING:

Peter caressed the likeness of his parents saying, "They were a beautiful couple cut down before they were allowed a life."

Phillip agreeing, "We will never know what it would be like having parents, we can't let them get away with that crap, not in my lifetime!" His anger was formidable.

The brothers hugged one another they pledged together, "We will uncover legally the leaders and the killer that gave the order to assassinate our parents, and why?" The twin's camaraderie and conversations were as easy as if they had been raised together over the years. They could rest their arm around each other's shoulder comfortably, as if that were an everyday occurrence.

Ten O'clock found them reading their folders comparing notes making plans and elaborating on their strong points. Peter said, "No one knows about us, they should never know about us right away We'll be the surprise .We should go at them from different sides striking at the same times."

Phillip said, "Sounds good I thought of that moments ago, see we are together." He was quiet several seconds, then asked, "...What type songs does Kassi sing?"

Peter answered, "Pretty much any kind, she was raised in a musical family, why?"

Phillip responded, "I own, or we, own Thunder Bay Lodge and Casino, I use singers often, we I need one now."

Peter said. "She has a backup group they are all singers in their own rights, I met her in Europe where they brought the house down because they do oldies and modern, an eclectic collection."

"Do you think she'll work for us, we would pay them well?" Phillip said.

Peter responded, "They are good business women, the group went through school together. Ask them, I can't speak for them."

Phillip said, "I need to get my experts together and you do the same, we can work together or independly... hit them the same times far apart."

Peter answered, "That's smart they don't know we exist and can confuse them, I like that brother. I'll meet you at say in the morning about ten?"

Phillip replied, "I will, we can stop for the night I'm bushed. We can't let these clowns get away with these murders, even though it's a twenty year old killings, I know people we can tap for gathering information. We are co-owners of DeHaven News Corporation, We'll get this done. We can't live in the Manor even though it's been refurbished." he closed his folder.

Peter leaned back in his seat saying, "While we grew up I had some of the damndest shocking waking dreams, but never knew what caused them. After reading these folders and our being conjoined twins I have a better idea of the cause. We grew up apart on different continents I have an English accent, yours is more American something that might keep us safe for a while anyway."

Phillip chuckled and said, "I had dreams of you and your pleasures, like dancing with girls, drinking parties I never could have done. My Aunt Abigail was a loud singer, she actually dressed me like a girl with long curls all in the name of saving me, and she called me her little Phillipa, among other things. She was as crazy as a lunatic 'till I was ten I stood up and refused to be her little Pillipa... I think I'll grow a mustache...what do you think?"

Peter answered, "A mustache would be good...We will have to correct that wardrobe..., I was a recipient of your pain and discomfort. Were you bitten by a dog on your arm?"

Phillip nods his head then said, "I was interested in a girl once but Aunt Abigail put an end to that, there were many things I could not do, she watched me all the time it was a kin to being in prison."

Peter said, "I felt your pain although I did not feel it constantly as you did in her presence."

Phillips voice mellowed said, "Aunt Abigail was as crazy as hell, she formed a crew of women, who looked like dock workers and fought like boxers, and they taught Special Ops in service...all in the name of keeping me safe." Phillip said laughing, "She said before she died her love for me was twisted love but it was genuine, her intentions were keeping me safe. Actually I had to be with her at all office meetings and read all the minutes. Now I appreciate her for doing all that. I appreciate them all, my sitters through the years I met with them and learned judo and other Marshall arts. I appreciate that."

There was a whirl wind of activities, ward robes, hair, makeup, rehearsals , signs and advertisement, all it takes to ready the singing group before opening night. His cell phone rang momentarily.

Phillip listened then answers. "Yes Joe?"

Joe said in an anxious voice," Joe here, we need to talk as soon as possible, you need to know what we found!"

PHILLIP said, "If it's that urgent come on over."

Joe asked "Can we meet tonight?" He said. "We need to talk tonight it can't wait>"?'

"I'll meet you in my office as soon as you can get here." Phillip answered.

JOE burst through the office door saying breathlessly. "Sir we have hit a big mess."...he opens the duffel bag filled with drugs. "The guy we followed was a Detective in our police force....very nervous, wet his pants. We followed him to the home of the Police Commissioner. My guys are watching them...several people went hurriedly into the P.C.s home tonight and they are still there."

The Thunder Bay Lodge and Casino, opening night, clever advertisement stimulated the public's imagination; outside showed the tastefully decorated entry as the guests arrived.

An adult cut out of Kassi Knight showed the lovely smiling KASSI KNIGHT well coifed, elegantly dressed in a black backless gown, slit up above one knee revealing her well turned long leg.

She danced saying on center stage, "Good evening Ladies and Gentlemen welcome to THUNDER BAY CASCINO, I am Kassi Knight here with my best friends to entertain you, let's get to it." As she danced to the rhythm, the music swelled in the background in her husky voice she said the night is young let's celebrate sing." CELEBRATION the strains of the song fade into the background.

Peter sat at ring side listening. Enjoying the moment.

Phillip in an alcove above the customers, his stare was drawn to a single man seated near Peter surreptitiously taking phone pictures. Phillip dialed Peter saying, into his cell phone when Peter picked up, Phillip said, "Just listened don't look around. You are being checked out, not to worry I've got this."
Phillip dialed again saying quietly "JOE?"
Response Joe said, "Yes sir, Joe speaking."

Phillip said, "Joe there is a man at table 32 , he's taking pictures of the customers get a copula guys, I want him followed wear your hoodeys, stage a fake robbery I want that camera, make it look good don't hurt him, take everything money, watch I want that camera. Can you do that, shake him up don't hurt him much then follow him scare the hell out of him let him get away, follow him. Can you do that?"
Joe said, "Piece of cake, I know just what to do leave it to me, sir."
Phillip said, "I want his driver's license, car registration', his destination, where he lives who lives with him the address where he works, who he works for, everything you consider helpful to me."

Hours later in a dark alley three men lounged waiting, soon the customer walks along talking on his cell phone, says. "Yes I have pictures ..." suddenly he stops speaking.

Number one lounger said, "Hey there, we have a need for a drink, how about being neighborly and loan us the money for drinks all around?"
The phone caller answered, "I can't help you I'm in a hurry." tried to walk away.
Number two said, "You didn't appear to be in a hurry, a while ago, come ooooonnnn you can spare enough for one little drink all around."
Number three saying, "He's not being neighborly, look at him he's not being neighborly he's stingy, or maybe he just not into us," number three continues, "Someone in our group he doesn't like, right feller?" and looks pointedly at the African American. Number three says, "That's it you don't like African Americans, is that it stingy, and are you a racist? Protect and serve don't you like your clause I think it's kind of catchy." slapped him from cheek to cheek, added, "That's what you are sport, a dirty racist. I like that watch." then hugged him roughly around his shoulders.

The captive started to cry and wet his pants.
His captors saw the urine and laughs, "You just hate African Americans...they are citizens, too."

The captives fear consumed him looking from one to the other nervously answered, "No I - I- fine I'm just in a, I'm in a hurry."

Number one said, "Hey let's try it, It should look great on African Americans the gold stands out." He removed the watch roughly... put it on his partner, stood back to admire his handy work, and said, "I was right, see my guy looks great in that watch."

Number three looks the automobile over inside and out, YOUR NAME IS SHARP AND YOU WORK FOR THE City and you are a cop, you're a good cop I hope., Oh well no matter cops count too."

Number two added, "What else do you have, oh man that wallet is the best leather, matches my new suit, and it has money, lots of money, and he said he didn't have any." he made tic tic noise said, "Shame on you, your mother let you lie like that, what else you have, is this your car?"

"Now that's a jazzy ride, I like it, goes with my new watch." Number three said.

Number one said, "Leave the man something he needs to go home and change his pants, have a heart, he can't walk around like that, all pissey..."

Number two, said, "Oh alright if I gotta, spoil sport I'll get the number just in case I need the car some day. Hey that's a nice bag I am leaving the car but I'm taking the bag. It goes with the new outfit I just decided to buy, and that's It no matter if he is a cop his money spends, one more thing what's in the bag?"

His partner started to speak.

The searcher held up a hand said, "I know, I'll stop, zip it... and to show you I am a sport I want even open it... I can wait." Laughing made the motion as if zipping his lips.

Number one says, "Oh damn it if you just gotta have something take the damn bag but nothing else." then said to Sharp, "...Get the hell outta here before I change my mind." The captive cop hesitates "Get the hell outta here ...go on get!"

The captive hurried away.

HOURS LATER:

SHARP dialed, said give me CHAMBERS, waits several moments, saying, "I was robbed of everything including the package. And you know we have to tell MR. BIGGARS, we all know his temper, he'll be pissed."

Chambers saying, "That's your next job telling him. I feel for you."

Office of BIGGARS his phone sounded... He enters during the ring...A large dog came happy to see him...the dog when on hind legs was as tall as his master...

Biggars said, "BOREGARD how you are old pal?" as he patted the Russian WOLF HOUND... The phone continues to ring, "...Gotta get the phone..." BIGGARS answers the cell phone irritable, "Yeah It's your dime... what!?"

His expensive suit was rumpled with cigar ash on the lapel. The latest from his tailor he always say I get the best for me, as he chews on his very expensive illegal cigar. His clothes appeared as though he had slept in them several days.

Sharp said, nervous," Sharp here....Sir there was a robbery tonight they got away with the merchandise the whole shipment before I could get to the destination."

"Who took it!? " Biggars yelled into the cell phone. Saying, "I want those professionals, mercenaries, I don't care about the cost...this shipment is the largest ever. For this major world cartel...I want them yesterday I don't care... I need to know what to tell the boss...Mr. DUNBAR will be pissed."

"It was three of them...all wore masks sir." Sharp answered.

"We got a leak obviously...." Maniacal laughter, "The last time there was leak like that...NOAH had a damn boat." more laugh, "Hell there was a leak like that and the damn TITANIC sank." Belly laugh

He stopped long enough to pet BOREGARD the big dog relaxing before the fireplace. . Biggar said, "I know there are at least two, things have been moved over the years...I believe those twins are alive and in the united States somewhere..."

."I want them found I want them Dead!!! You understand! Find their families...I want them dead!" Biggars yelled again,

Boregard sits to attention every time his master yells...he settles down when he finds Biggars was not really angry enough, he sits to attention with every shout from Biggars.

BIGGARS continued, "Find their animals I want them dead! Burn their houses down to the ground!! If you can't find them you're in trouble with me understood... get a move on FIND THEM!!!??" He smashed the cell phone against the wall.

He stormed around the room kicking tables over muttering sometimes low and at times yelled loudly. "I have A Major Cartel waiting for this shipment... the most I ever put together... I'll cover America ... better still I'll have the whole planet shaking on dope," more laughter. A knock at the door stopped him short of laughing, his voice suddenly changed. His face was cunning and sneaky, Biggars whispering laughing maniacally,

Boregard leaves the room...

A little person dusted the hall tables... listening to every shouted word.

Biggars continues, "I'll have millions... some poor sucker tries to mess up my plans… but not this time" he kicks over another table and chair, the room is a wreck.

Biggars dialed his phone, saying "its Biggars…someone took the nights shipment…I am working on a way to find it."

The phone crackled an answer."

Biggers said."I'm on it…I still think it's those DeHaven twins…" the phone crackled again, "I know not again…the twins are somewhere in this." Slammed the phone down.

Servants stood outside wide eyes and afraid…

Finally MORGAN the man servant knocks softly on the door saying."MORGAN here, sir."

BIGGAR in a changed friendly voice said, "Yes come in MORGAN."

Joe walked pass the adult cut out of Kassi Knight, he listened to the swinging music momentarily. Gave Kassi the double thumbs up as he continued to the offices.

Inside Phillips office Joe shrugged out of the knapsack to those present saying. "I thought we all needed to know what we're up against." He opened the bag to show the narcotics.

They gathered around to view the cache of drugs Joe said,

'We thought it was safe to follow anyone who belonged to this shipment. It really led to some interesting people and places."

Joe paused, then continued, "I'll just tell it all save time anyone can jump in as they see fit. "He paused then, said, 'First he visited his home he pissed his pant when we intimidated him, can you imagine, a Police detective wetting his pants?"

Laughter. "He had to go home to change…then he went to home of the POLICE CHEIF…and the surprise of them all." C.E.O. of Sellers Conglomerate and the POLICE COMMISSIONER of this city… AN UNKNOWN FIGURE ENTERED the backdoor… couldn't tell who it was… "

Music is heard with audience appreciation; he closed the door and the music can barely be heard.

He said, "We stopped the guy who took pictures, these were taken of Peter, we have pictures of almost every one there. "Joe spread everything in the bag on the table.

JOSH said, "We've got some heavy hitters just in the group we observed tonight. We need to get our self together and find out what's going on… this could be a huge operation."

"We need to get together… we have a lot of work cut out for us, we can meet at the Eagles Laire tomorrow night after nine o'clock. I'll put this bag away for safe keeping. Be sure and get CLARENCE and his wife CLARISSA their sons OTTO and OMAR… they have photographic memories…whizzes with anything to do with computers one family of the little people both parents are sharp shooter , they have other skills, too… like lips readers, a lot of skills we can use from their carnival days. I'll see everybody back here tomorrow. We need them … I have someone to walk home, see you tomorrow."

He leaves the office ahead of the group with the bag he stored in the safe.

The background music swells as they leave… the sounds a rousing Conga line, whistles and audience applause.

Phillip and LEYLA YOUNG arrived at her apartment. They paused Phillip turned to her saying shyly, "I've walked you home several times, I think it would be nice to kiss you good night."

Leyla answered, "Sure I've wondered about that myself … lay one on me."

He held her in his arms kissed her lightly on the lips.

Leyla encircled her arms around his neck and kissed him soundly on the mouth. He felt her heart beat against his chest, and the warmth of her soft body as it touched the erogenous points as it molded against him… they were lost in their all consuming desire.

Phillip backed away and whispered, "You should go inside." Her fragrance was overwhelmingly intoxicating…

Leylas skin seemed to have been touched by the Hawaiian sun as she grew up.

She answered, "We should take this up later."

"I'll call you tomorrow," he replied.

"If a man answers… hang up." She answered laughing.

Phillip smiling said, "YEAH…RIGHT…see you tomorrow."

Leyla backed away…then turned and walked away.

He watched her ample bosom as she backed away, and turned… showing neat waist to her flaring hips, her swaying voluptuous body until she was safe inside the apartment before he turned to leave. Saying, "Thanks Aunt Abigail for saving me for something better … Wow." there's pep in his steps, a smile on his face.

Phillip lies in bed between sleep and wakefulness.

A mist forms in the far corner of the room, out of the mist Aunt Abigail materializes smiling, there is no fear for Phillip.

The figure speaks saying, "I watched over you and kept you safe, you didn't come with instructions I had to improvise many times …I ask you never hate, it's like a poison that grows out of the ground in our country. My love for you was twisted but here you are, ready to face the dangers of life. I kept you safe. You are with your brother, and have the right woman. I can rest now…rest…rest." As Abigail fades into the mist.

Police noises outside Sharps office.

Detective Sharp spoke into his phone, saying" I met your Mr. Biggars I must say he's a frustrated old man… should be a registered nut. He thinks there are two people watching him…
Boregard the dog told him so."
"Yes I've known him several years and every time I see him I want to kill him." the caller said laughing.
"I know the feeling, I talk to him for a few minutes and I wanted to kill him, too." Both laugh.
"Biggar is needed; he's a genius at what he does believe me even though he acts as crazy as hell."

Kassis bedroom…Peter is in bed alone, heard singing and used his cell phone dialed put it on speaker…, when answered he asked, "Where are you? Were you singing? I miss your warm body near me."
Kassi answers, "Yes, it was me… I like that song …I'm in the kitchen …getting your breakfast…" she is wearing a midriff top, hot pants and a tiny apron.
"You don't cook…where did you get my breakfast… and what's for breakfast?" Peter replied amazed.
She answers, "You'll know when you eat it…"
Peter said, "Guessing game before breakfast."
"I ordered three kinds…looks good…Ham and eggs…bacon and eggs, and sausage and eggs…warm buttered toast, jam, marmalade…hot coffee I think I ordered all the fixing… all in the warmer" Kassi responded pleased with herself…she thought for seconds then asked, "Where are you calling from?"
Peter answers, "From the bedroom where else…come in here I have something to tell you."
Moments later, Kassi danced into the bedroom to the music 'IN THE MOOD' she said."I was busy … What do you want to tell me?"
He raised the covers, saying "Hop in here and I'll tell you…" Peter continues, "Remember I told you we are getting married… because I love you, and I want you near me…I need … no I can't get enough of your touch…?"
Kassi nods… removes the tiny apron… revealing hot pants sleep wear, and midriff top… as she climbed into bed.
"Sweetheart cooking is not your strong suit…and not why I am marrying you…I need you rested and beautiful… and other enticements."
Kassi asked, "…and you called me from the bedroom to the kitchen,

two rooms away... to tell me you were lonely?"

Peter said, "Yes... you shouldn't leave me... for a heart attack on toast... I wanted you here because I love you.... And I'm lonely when you're not with me and, you don't cook."

Kassi saying, "I know I don't cook... proud of it, babe...I ordered breakfast just for you... from 'THUNDER BAYs KITCHENS'."

"Were you ever told not to come to bed in so many clothes... less struggle under the covers?"Peter asked.

Kassi answers, as she snatched the breakaway hot pants off, saying "Oh you mean this old thing?" holding up the hot pants.

Peter said, "I didn't want your warm spot to cool...I saved it for you... and I missed your soft, warm body near me... I was lonesome... you can sing just for me anytime... I like that."

"So you were lonely... You nut I was busy getting your breakfast!"... Kassi hit him with a pillow...the pillow fight began...laughing they ended in each other's arms...to love making...breakfast forgotten.

DAYS LATER:

The groups were assembled in the conference room at the Eagles Laire,

Dr. Morton said, "Thanks for coming... we have a lot to discuss... I'll make this quick...you can add later." He pauses then said. "This all started twenty years ago with the murders of Carter and Caroline's deaths... We had to get the twins out of harm's way to prevent them being killed, we gave them the time to grow up... and a chance to defend themselves. This is PHILLIP and PETER DeHaven those babies of over twenty years ago." Late comers walk in...

The leader said, "I am CLARENCE, my wife CLARRISA, two of my sons OTTO and OMAR...and last with us are IDA, BERTHA and MARTHA...our neighbors."

Dr. Morton continues, saying, "You all know everyone...

We should get down to the business...at hand..."

Phillip and Peter listened and took notes.

Dr, Morton said, "Our new comers have Intel that's important for us to start.... I'll ask Clarence...to tell us what he and his family have done so far."

Clarence said, "We have been able to check into their computer systems... walked through the caves in the many small alcove openings... we can do it that way due to our size and take photographs...my sons have the ability to read lips, in the last few days we have planted listening devises in the homes and offices."

Peter asked, "How did you do all this in such a short time?"

"We are little people not noticed throughout societies...our size is on our sides... called Midgets, Dwarfs etc. ...not noticed in most societies ...

My wife and I are sharp shooters, Marshall artists… you get the picture… listen to this… we over heard Biggars yelling,.. I'll put it on speaker."

Biggars voice filled the room… 'I want you to find their dogs I want them dead'… burn their houses down to the ground.'

'Clarence said, "Give us more time we will get more."

JOE asked," We're here why? They were unborn babies? That's a hell-a-way to grow up and find a sentence of death over your head."

Another spoke, "Who? Could do this to babies?"

Dr. Morton answered, "Before Abigail died she found …there are caves under DeHaven land connecting to the entries under SELLERS property… they were used in the past by gun runners, during prohibition, slavery and later, Rum runners over the years. That area is very stable …earthquakes never damaged them… they are strong."

Phillip said, "Can you get more photographs…give us a better sense of what we're dealing with?"

Clarence continues, "Abigail found the caves… they are being used now for the illegal drug trade a very lucrative business enterprise… the business by a dangerous bunch of murderers they kill everything in sight if needed… it will take no how, plus an army to get rid of them… they are covered by money men"

JOE said, "According to the handouts … the caves covers a large area."

CLARENCE, one of the little people from Abigail's colony a sharp shooter from his younger years was tall for a small person… he added to his height with lifts on his shoes and cowboy boots.

Everyone shuffled through the packets to find the photographs.

Clarence continuing, said "My children played on the bluff overlooking Sellers Estate…they could see lights moving in and out the darkness…and later my wife and I took a look and saw trucks drive in and out of the caves especially…we kept our eyes on them and found why… Some of the rooms under DeHaven land are huge caves carved by nature over centuries."

Joe interjected, "Anything for the almighty drugs."

DR. Morton said, "Now if you want to read through your folders we will answer your question… until we have more Intel… we're playing catch up."

Noises of the busy police department are heard… the ringing of phones, a drunken party goers sing off key in the drunk tank… sober prisoners yell for the singers to "shut up"! … Police bring new prisoners in hand cuffs, yelling 'police brutality… Sergeant I didn't do anything'…

chairs scrape the floor...cell doors clang shut...several officers stick a finger in the ears trying to hear the caller on the phones... a fight breaks out between prisoners who were arrested fighting on the streets.

Detective Sharp said into the cell phone. "Did you hear Biggars Dog, Boregard... whoever killed the dog dressed him in a trench coat, hat and boots... police are there now we just heard the call... they are telling Biggars about now."

The Detective answered, "Yes and the nut will crack, he probably will continue to talks to Boregard...his dead bosum buddy." Both laughed and broke the connection.

Morgan the houseman entered Biggars' library hurriedly, saying "Sir we have a problem...please come its urgent!!!" He waited momentarily to catch his breath, said "its BOREGARD sir we found him dead on the cliffs." Then ran out, followed by Biggars', servants and visitors...

The RUSSIAN WOLFE HOUND was tied to a Gazebo Post dressed in a hat, trench coat and boots. From one angle it appeared to be a dead man... from his front showed the large dog.

Biggars almost fainted; Morgan had to help him to a seat. The dog's owner was so over come he needed a moment to recover from his shock. Before the dog was cut down, one read the note tied around Boregards neck that read, "Your dog first... you're next we'll meet soon."

His owners face soften when he sat beside Boregard's body... he said, as he touched the dogs head saying. "I am sorry it had to be you. You rest feller you gave me love and understanding, rest on old friend." he covered Boregards head gently.

Turning to those gathered near he said, "We have people to see. Things to do." His old grumpy self again, "WE have work to do... get a move on! Whoever did this will pay!" he rushed into the house and slammed the door.

Everyone was fascinated with the spectacle until Morgan and servants cut the body down and wrapped, and put in a suitable receptacle ready for burial in the estates animal cemetery

Midnight finds Biggar beside Boregards grave. He said, "Well big feller...it's just you and me now ...you were the greatest companion and friend. There are those working against me...things disappear ...I know there are two of them. I have an order in for the professional... the real Mercenaries...those guys kill for the joy of killing ... you're the first to know boy." Boregards picture showed the dog as he appeared in life.

Biggars said, "I'll be lost without you." A tear rolled down his cheek.

His cell phone sounded Biggars answered gruffly, "Biggars speaking, what? "

A voice said, "I've kept eyes on the Thunder Bay Casino and Inn, I've found the owner has a close look at some of your movements, it would be to your benefit to take a look...check it out, the owner has the hots for one of the backup singers." the caller broke the connection.

Biggars looked at the phone... Laughing said, "I knew there were two... I think those twins have survived...grown up and are here...you are the only one who believes me ole boy" he pressed the intercom button saying. "Morgan get them all in here please."

The POLICE COMMISSIONER GORDON entered first, saying "How are you Biggars and Boregard today?"

The Police Commissioner. is tall once handsome with his good looks disappearing along with his waistline, but still dresses well... there is indications of his heavy drinking, by the hands tremors and his red nose... he went to the bar and pour a tall drink. Saying "I'll be glad when this is all over... if you want my opinion..."

Biggars interrupted said angrily, "When I want your opinion I'll give you one...now just sit back drink your drink and listen."

If possible the Police Commissioner turned even redder....looks around sheepishly then sat quietly down.

Biggars continues, "Gordon I am well if you must know... Boregard is still dead... I am not as nutty as you think...Boregard is a habit that I continue to speak to." His voice is clear and business like. He said, "I am glad you're still here...we need to talk about the coming week."

One asked, "Then we're ready ...what about guards...how do we protect the shipments?"

Biggars answered, "I'm glad you ask SAM... We are about to embark on the biggest shipment ever....I have tanker ships....helicopters, and trucks all ready to deliver to our overseas counterpart... it will rain enough drugs down to satisfy every taste...."

Sam asked, "What about boots on the ground we need them, too?"

"They're beginning to filter into town ...I contacted Merck's...black Ops...ex-Navy seals...plain ole crooks... these... if I can call them People... kill anything on the planet and some not nailed down... we'll have money hand over fists as rich as any ole money bags. "

The Police Commissioner said, "You seem to have everything covered... If you think of anything more you need give me a call...I'll be waiting...I have to go now a meeting at city hall."

Biggars said, "Just so you know commissioner....Boregard and I took a flight by helicopter after the first two robberies ... and there is no way one person could be forty miles away and commit those hold ups....I've maintained there are two leaders... those are the DeHaven twins I haven't seen them but they're here and grown up."

The Police commissioner tipped his forehead as he left the room.

Kassi Knight on stage moving to the rhythm of the music said, "Thanks for being here it's no fun without you... now it is time for us to say good night...but first let's have a last dance up close and personal with whatever BOO you're with... I am...." Lights dimmed...

Peter comes forward takes Kassi in his arms and moves slowly up close and very personal. He whispers, "I am here up close and personal as suggested," she cradled her head on his shoulder.

They dance barely moving until lights out.

The phone in Clarence's office sounded, he answers saying, "Engels speaking."

OTTOS voice fill his ear...said quietly, "Dad...we are in the Caverns now...there are hidden alcoves... we can see almost everything... there are workmen, all over...in the offices... this place is huge...larger than we first thought."

Omar continues, "This is a huge enterprise out of sight.... Dad we're looking at an enormous supply of drugs... more than we have ever seen in one place hundreds of kilos. This covers everything....offices, the whole enterprise it's all here collected in this one spot...we need more time to take a look at it all."

CLARENCE frightened said, "Come home... and you be careful some people like them can be killers... I don't want you on a slab in the morgue... come home now!"

Omar said, "Dad...We ran into this guy we know...he's at our place flying high as a kite... we'll have more to tell as soon as he comes down from cloud nine..."

Otto laughing saying "Yeah dad he's really out of sight."

Otto and Omar are Clarence's sons all members of the little people compound....both sons are computer geniuses, can read lips, and has a photographic memory for everything they hear or read..."

It is evening...the DeHaven twins group is gathered in the conference room at EAGLE LAIRE... Doctor Morton stood at the head of the conference table saying, "We can get to the evenings work... there's a lot to do ... we will start with CLARENCE ENGELS...Clarence you're up."

Clarence is the leader of the little people... stands erect at five feet tall....dresses meticulously and wears cowboy boots with built up heels and soles. He said, "Our compound was built by Abigail in the trees overlooking the waterfall, the lagoon and a portion of the Sellers property."

Dr.Morton interrupted said, "Get to the point ...seeing the lights and other movement."

Clarence said more quickly, "Oh yeah, weeks ago my children were playing on the cliffs at dust and saw lights mostly from trucks and men working ....My wife and I walked along where the lights had been seen and recorded trucks going into and out of caverns in the cliffs... we could not see them from the ocean side nor could we go in the vicinity by day."

PHILLIP from the back of the room asked, "Did you ever inspect the area...what did you find? We know they will lash out at anyone who might try to stop them..."

Peter continues saying, "We must caution you all... these are desperate people who will kill you... I can't caution you anymore than to say... be careful... be suspicious of anyone you don't know... especially the police."

Clarence answered, " Yes....the whole area is honey comb with caves as big as living rooms tunnels like large hallways... some are enormous and trucks can be parked inside out of sight I have pictures. There are rooms filled with office files, papers and stacks of drugs in spaces just for that, more than I've seen in one place....it boggles the mind ... we didn't have time to find more... some members of my family work for the Sellers... some of us ... especially my sons....read lips and we have listening devices throughout the home....you can read the hand outs for the rest."

Dr. Morton said, " This all started over twenty years ago...Sellers wanted to buy DeHaven property because most of the large caves are under DeHaven Manor...Carter would not sell... the reason his pregnant wife and he were murdered... almost killed the DeHaven twins."

Joe asked, "How long have these caves' been known about?"

Dr. Morton answered, "As far back as slavery, then rum runners, now we have the mega drug traders and they are ahead of us...we have catching up to do... Nature has not affected the caverns' probably before time began and especially earthquakes...never affected them."

Clarence saying, " We little people have many ways to get Intel some of us read lips, also there are listening devices that we have modified... we have walked the caverns and have a better idea of what is going on... we have expertise in weaponry and can teach everyone who needs it..."

Dr. Morton said, "Abigail built the LITTLE PEOPLES COMPOUND in the trees. The living quarters are in the trees and the stores , restaurants, theatres, school from K-to nine everything to do with commercialism in the lower buildings it's a small city of its own...go and see it."

Clarence added, " Your door key is one... the other in your packets... my sons OTTO, and OMAR are expert in miniaturizing the modern communication systems...we have equipped all our living quarters with devices to alert our families when something happens, we will do yours ... now I'm done." Clarence sat.

Dr. Morton said, "You all have burner phones and g-mail go home get acquainted with your packets, learn them commit them to memory, then destroy them..."

'Sound out your surroundings report anything out of the ordinary to me, Phillip or Peter...or squad leaders... we have detected what is known as the shadow squad following most of us so be aware of those around us ... stay safe."

CLARENCE added, "Thanks doc for that...We will add some safe guards to your homes alarm systems...If there is an invasion we all will know about it... for safety...we will find you...there will be hidden cameras scattered throughout you homes we'll know who and when they broke in and what they did..."

Otto spoke saying, "My brother Omar and I have shortened the time for tracing in coming phone calls...we cut down to less than three minutes tops right now."

OMAR continued said, "Jewelry for women and buttons, belt buckles... and other little baubles...we have several more things... miniaturizing is one of our specialties...we have many such things."

"My brother and I ran into someone who is usually out of this world... from sampling the goods." Otto added.

Omar laughs saying, "He's usually high on the product ... we're waiting for him to come back down to earth again ... we can tell you more... we need to go and check on him." As they leave the room.

TEN DAYS LATER:
In Phillips office at the door to the outside.

He said softly, "Angel face...Joe will drive you home tonight and see you to the door... You have your key given to you by Clarence?"

Leyla answered, "Yes...right here." Showed the key.

He said, "Good... I want you to save this for me."and kissed her soundly on the mouth then spanked her playfully on her fanny, saying ,"This too... like that CHARLEY PRIDE song, KISS AN ANGEL IN THE MORNING that's you " Then whispers "You are my Angel face,"

Leyla laughing said, as she opened the car door, "For you...all is possible." She threw a kiss and joined Joe.

Phillip leaned out the door saying, "Joe is careful that's precious cargo."

They both smiled and waved goodbye.

Biggars, into his cell phone, saying "I want no more pussy footing around, I want the gal pal in my cabin in the woods by morning…I'll be there later…I want her able to talk… understand. She probably has information I want, or her disappearance will get it from the man friend… tonight!" he emphasized slamming the phone down on his desk…he made another call, saying to the person that answered, "We are down to the second shipment… everything is going bad I mean right now." He

Stopped talking momentarily then said, "…how could we be so wrong…?"

Peter awoke…heard singing from a distance…felt for Kassi then dialed the phone… when answered saying. "Were you singing…Where are you?"

Kassi replied, "Yes that was me singing…I am in the kitchen getting your breakfast."

Peter thought for seconds then said. "Would you come here a moment…I have something to tell you…" says to himself softly. "If she's cooking I'll know when the smoke alarm goes off…, "

Kassi her complexion a coffee and cream glowed in the morning light…she danced in to the music 'IN THE MOOD' she came into the room in minutes… stopped with her hands on her hips wearing a tiny apron over hot pants sleep wear…"I'm here… what can I do for you, sir?"

Peter amused… likes the wearing apparel, raised her side of the coverlet said. "Hop in here I'll tell you."

Kassi complied removed the apron, said, "Okay …I'm here what do you want to tell me…?"

He kissed her face lovingly "Uuuuuummm You taste like coffee…Do you remember when I said we are getting married?"

Kassi Nods.

He continues…"What are you cooking?"

"You'll know when you eat it… I just stored it in the warmer…Bacon and. eggs ham and eggs, and sausage and eggs….hot coffee buttered toast and other things…you'll love it."

He said. "Sweet heart… I am not marrying you for your cooking skills… remember you can't cook. I wll hire the cooks… you will not need to stand over a hot stove for me… get all tired… did anyone ever tell you not wear all those clothes to bed?"

Kassi yanked the breakaway hot pants for sleep off, saying "You mean this old thing? I never told you I could cook…who ever told you that… lied… I ordered breakfast from Thunder Bay kitchen… they had your favorites."

Peter replied. "You get my meaning…you could even come to bed without any thing…less struggling under the covers. "

"Oh you are not funny."Hit him with a pillow…the pillow fight was on with laughing and falling down in bed…. The fight turned to love making… and sleep… breakfast was forgotten.

Three men in hoods' and masks crept through the evening shadows rang the door bell using Phillips special ring.

Leyla sets her glass on the table hurries to open the door saying, "Honey did you change your plans...?" opens the door. ...
The leader shoves her into the apartment roughly said, "No bitch... honey is not here...where did he go?"
Leyla scurries back to reach her phone but nervously knocked everything off the table which activated the hidden alarm systems...

Clarence's team members drop whatever they were doing and assembled at the designated spot...watched over hidden cameras as the intruders tore Leylas home apart room by room...
The leader slaps Leylas across her face until she fell on the floor.
Another masked man lifted Leylas limp body off the floor, saying "Stop... you could kill her you know Biggars will be pissed...you don't want that with him... let's take her to the cabin, revive her and question her there."

Cell phones with special alarms sounded.

Kassi heard the report went to her closet undressing on the way...
Shortly she emerged from her bedroom wearing form fitting leather... her Glock 9mm low on her hip. Rifle in a leather carrying case.
Peter looked at her clothes asked, "Where are you going?"
Kassi answered, "To get Leyla...let's go times wasting."
Peter answered laughing;"...You're packing can you use that thing?"
"Wait and see...come on honey... let's go...don't worry about me."Kassi replied.
Peter drove away.

Sellers Cabin in the woods on his property...

Peter led the rescuers as they crept quietly.
Two guards were silently put in a choke hold after a struggle... they were rendered unconscious lowered to the ground...
Peter the rescue leader indicated by pointing the way they were to cover the cabin...front and back.

Leyla blindfold was tied to a chair in the middle of a large room.

One kidnapper asks loudly. "Where did he go!?"
Leyla crying in pain answered, "I don't know!"

The questioner slapped her across the face, saying, "You're sleeping with him…don't you have pillow talk? After sweating between the sheets with him?"

"I don't know anything about his business." Leyla cried.

The kidnapper drew back his hand to strike her again…

The door burst open followed by Peter gun drawn said, "Do that…" the kidnapper reached toward the table…Peter continuing saying,"…and draw back a stump." He was followed by, Kassi Knight and his groups from three directions.

The kidnapper said, "Come any closer she no longer breathes on this earth." He reached toward the detonator on the table nearby.

Kassi aiming her Glock 9 MM at the kidnaper saying, "…Don't touch that …big mistake."

The kidnaper laughed saying, "You got your daddy's gun what ca…"

Kassi said, "Can you see this," fires blowing the kidnapers eye out…his brain and blood spattered on the wall.

Peter turned in surprise, said "Oh baby… you get my attention."

The other rescuers went to the last two kidnappers Kassi and Peter released Leyla, carefully unties her removing the blind fold ….helping her to walk.

Peter called Phillip when he heard rapid gun fire in the background… he grimaced in pain as he felt the sharp tearing impact, and the pain in his flank and shoulder, he bent over in momentary agony.

Kassi asked anxiously, "What's wrong?"

Peter dialed Phillip saying "Phillip has been wounded… I need to talk to him now." Paused then said, "Phil are you alright I felt the hits."

"Hell no…I've been shot! shoulder and flank… Its flesh wounds and it really hurts like hell…okay. How is my angel face is she okay?"

"The kidnappers were a tad bit rough with her… Doctor is on his way now, to meet us at the Laire…she fainted in the car … Kassi is holding her in the back seat… Hidden cameras Clarence installed works great… the kidnappers tore her place apart." Peter said.

Phillip said anxiously, "I'm on my way." He rolled off the examining table and shrugged one arm into his blood stained shirt, saying to Clarence and one of his men, "Drive me to the Laire."

Peter said, "Kassi and I are with her, take your time… trust me we shared a womb at one time… be careful" Peter trying for amusement.

Phillip answered. "I don't doubt you…I am coming… on my way now womb buddies." Phillip hurries out to the waiting car.

Kassi asked, "What happened to you…when you grimaced seemingly in pain?"

Peter answered, "We are twins joined at the head and scapular and by a fluke of nature we feel each other's pains or pleasures."

Kassi smiled and said, "Bully for you...you can keep tabs on each other." She said with sass."

Phillip rushes into the clinic... Peter and Kassi are aghast at his bloody shirt....

But Phillip has eyes only for Leyla saying, "Look what they did to my angel."

She wore an eye patch covering a black eye, bruising on that side of the face... a swollen and split lower lip... she was connected to oxygen, her heart monitor beat at a steady rate has a steady cadence, I.V. fluid drip and her feet were elevated ... there were ligature marks rubbed raw from being tied too tight on both wrists and ankles she was as quiet as death.

Dr, Morton entered, saying "Phillip it's not as bad as it looks...I am being careful on the safe side.... We are trying to save the baby."

Peter and Kassi did a quick inhale in surprise.

Phillip is surprised...asked, "A baby...what happened doctor?" he sits beside her bed held her hand gently in his..A pained look on his face.

Dr. Morton said, "The usual way ...you make love one or several times then eventually there's a baby...She had to be struck on her abdomen...I keep her feet elevated to help stop the bleeding...I will not do surgery yet... we'll give the body time to heal... nurses around the clock will keep an eye on her...I'll keep her in an inducted sleep for as long as it takes... Leyla is strong and healthy, she'll be fine... I will do my damndest that baby will be, too... De ja vu all over again... I was here for Caroline... your mother"

Peter's cellphone sounds, he answers, listens, and then says to Phillip "Gotta go...now that I see you're okay... they've got Biggars men cornered..., seriously... Kassi I can't persuade you to stay here, they're doing some serious fighting."

Kassi said, "Nope I am going with you." then saying playfully. "You need my protection... we're a team don't you know that by now?

Dr. Morton asked, "Phillip...how are you doing?"

Phillip replied, "Its manageable Doc. . .... the wound is a through and through."

Doctor Morton said, "You be careful out there."

PHILLIP said," That makes the three of us...Doc. Take care of my angel... I am going to see this through...I'll need a shirt." One last look at Leyla...with caution changed into the clean shirt.

A nurse took the blood stained shirt.

Peter answers, equally as playful "Oh alright... come on... my pistol packing woman… and womb buddy. We're definitely a team; I don't want either of you hurt… now that I've found you both."

"Let's go…I've got your back." Kassi said. Goes to the door saying "Well… are you coming?"

Peter shrugs in surrender…leaves reluctantly.

Biggar fly over the first delivery truck…he saw crowds of law enforcement and truck drivers with their hands raised in surrender… he turns to fly home…. The cell sounded Biggars said, "Not now our plans have gone bad, and really bad …it's happening now!" Clicked off.

He rushed into the library shouted at Morgan, "I want you to notify number two delivery that the CIA and DEA is there at the docks…turn around… use the alternate route."

Morgan said, "It's too late sir…DEA, CIA, local police and other law enforcement officers have rounded them up and confiscated the load now, ex-seals and black Ops swarmed the freighter, from the air and under the sea and have taken that shipment… they have arrested the ship's crew…it's over."

"We have to save the third shipment…or this has been all for nothing… we've lost everything… I want let that happen." He went to his gun cabinet …

The door opens followed by F.B.I., other Law enforcements, Peter, Kassi and Phillip, arm in a sling who said quietly, "This is over Biggars… twenty years in the making… give it up you've lost."

Biggars turns and fires wildly…striking Kassi in her shoulder…her body twists around falls heavily against the wall…

Peter returns fire striking Biggars in the knee his leg collapses…

Peter went to help Kassi. He said, "We have to get you to a doctor."

Kassi saying, "It's just a scratch, I'll use the napkins at the bar… I need to see how this turns out…remember I have your back."

Peter with one finger under her chin tipped her face up looking at all angles lovingly …answered softly saying. "I love you …you're my pistol packing mama… I want you to stay that way, alive…Not this time…you will go and have the doctor look at that shoulder…no ifs, ands or buts about it you 'will" ..Go with Jerry and right now… now go." He spoke with authority… kissed her softly on the lips.

Kassi smiles saying, "My man …I love it when you take charge… Okay I'll go …it hurts like hell anyway." Jerry helps her out.

They passed Ida, Bertha and Martha on the way inside.

Ida asked, "Who did you shoot this time… you old fart?"

Phillip said, "You were right Biggars there are… two of us… plus three… and here they are."

Peter finished for Phillips, saying, " We are the DeHaven twins … the ones you almost murdered before we were born…all for DeHaven land…and by the way the overseas cartel has been taken over by Law Enforcement there… you're done."

"Why don't you just kill me…? Shoot me go ahead… shoot me… why is this happening to me." Biggars asked holding his wounded knee.

"…Because you've lived a life of crime…and now you're caught in a compromising position… get over it, it was your way or no way… I repeat get over it you old fart." Martha said.

"We can't do that… Killing you would be too easy…there are more things to show you… you and your co conspirators robbed us of a mother and father we can never know them…but we can avenge them within the law." Phillip pointed out.

Martha responding, "Like how did your dog die…and who did it…"

Biggers cried saying, "You bitch you killed my dog!"

Bertha laughing, said, "No not me…didn't think of it."

Ida replied, "Boregard had no pain… Biggar, do you remember saying during one of your tirades…and I quote…'I want them all dead… and you specified find their dog I want them all dead" I liked your suggestion…you got your wish."

Martha said, "In reality you killed your dog… jackass… you yelled it."

Biggars sobbed for Boregard, "Just kill me… I can't face this… there are spies in my home…everywhere!!" he grabs his injured knee in pain.

Bertha laughing saying, "We have to wait…you have a very large trial to go through dummy …along with your sister…how does it feel … was it all worth that…well you old sadist. You got what's coming to you… everything… all your plans down the preverbal drain."

The Police Commissioner was shoved in the door …and pushed into a chair…

An F.B.I., agent said, "Along with the unknown Mr. DUNBAR…"

Biggars, still holding his knee responded, "My sister, from another mother the planner of the whole scheme." His voice was all business.

Peter said, "The infamous three musketeers… we knew about you Mr. Dunbar but your indent was well hidden."

Dunbar reached up and striped the hat off … red hair tumbled out to her shoulders….She said. "I know you didn't see me…I was always among you…Biggars, my brother is a master of miss direction…talking to his dead dog…going on long tirades…acting out of his mind…he is a master of the fact that he can cloud your mind…" his sister takes a bow.

Biggars added, "My sister… Chemist, herbalist whatever you need… The chemist can formulate anything tasteless, odorless, any deadly… mind numbing drug you want…"

"We have something to cloud your minds"… Phillip replied "My brother along with European cartels …but you will recognize them… agencies that reached as far as other continents… we are not as backward as you think we are."

"…And the home grown can boggle your minds… believe it." Peter added.

K.I.S.G. Craig Gebhardt… with the days breaking news…, on the screen now you see the the efforts of multiple law agencies, working together to stop the flow of drugs worldwide. Ladies and gentlemen you are looking at the biggest drug bust ever seen." In the background Law enforcements are gathering the captives in police vans.

A crowd is coming from all around. The crowds of looky loos are watching showing all emotions awe, anger, shouting epitaphs.

Doctor Morton finished his examination of Kassi… he said, "You and leyla have joined the most prolific family of hormones…"

Kassi asked, "What does that mean Doctor?"

"You are both pregnant…will deliver about the same time…that is very interesting." Dr. Morton said.

Peter called by phone. Kassi answered, "You know what you've done to me?"

Peter responded, "What else could I have done but got you pregnant…" he replied with a smile.

Kassi said," Exactly… how did you know?"

"Remember I said Phillip and I enjoy pleasure and pain… I am glad… the pleasure was all mine…I loved it, and I'll do it again." Peter said laughing.

Kassi laughing saying, "Me, too…I'll let you… you devil."

"You get better we have two ceremonies to perform…bye, see you in a bit." Peter replied.

THIS IS JACK NORRIS with today's breaking news… There is media from all over the world converging in the city of NEW BOSTON…There is a problem with the jury pool… because of the wide spread news coverage… where to find a jury that can judge fairly?"

Reporters, camera men, sound vans all their equipment Computers and those with the ability to get the stories out in milliseconds… modern day news in seconds to all the corners in far away continents…They are reporting the news of the enormous task to saturate the world with drugs…

Citizens on the streets are stopped and asked about the perpetrators...

Asking...Did they know them, go to school with them, in business with them...

Did they know about them over twenty years, how could they not know with tons of all drugs being grown and transported through the city...?

Did they know about the DeHaven murders twenty years ago... with the constant threat on unborn, and growing babies heads...in that they had to be kept safe from the killers

...Phillip and Peter the actual twins involved were interviewed ... telling about never having parents and just finding one another after twenty years...not having a brother to be raised with. Along with employees, Doctors, nurses...

The story of Biggars tirades and talking to his dead dog, the discovery of his sister by another mother...

This is JACK NORRIS... KISG will tap in on the breaking news as it happens."

Philip sits beside Leylas hospital bed holding her hand...fell asleep... her hand movement to squeeze his hand...he awoke stared at her...then called, "Nurse I think she's waking."

The nurse came to take the patients' blood pressure, pulse, temperature readings said, "All good...I'll call Doc. Morton right away."

Doctor Morton arrives in minutes of the call, did a quick assessment, looked at the chart, and said "I think she's out of danger... I'll remove this equipment... except I want her legs elevated for at least twelve hours to make sure the bleeding has stopped, along with the eye patch stays..."

Leyla spoke. Saying "Thanks Doctor...I was beginning to think I was in a cocoon..."

"I have an idea of how you feel... guess who is here." The doctor said.

"Hi honey. The eye patch is a good idea makes me feel like one eyed Jack... in a good way."Leyla said.

Phillip answered, "The eye patch could be a fashion statement ...You are alive the most important... We have a few things to discuss when you're feeling better."

"Does it have anything to do with my being pregnant...I thought that was just in my dreams...I was not unconscious ...it was like a twilight sleep I could still hear people around me talking." Leyla replied.

The trial of the century begins for the top planners of the crimes... people gathered at the court building as early as four in the morning...the court fill to capacity within moments of the doors opening.

Clerk called Court to order, by, saying."Here yea...hear yea... this court will come to order ...the Honorable JUDGE ALMA LIONES presiding...

A middle aged ...grandmotherly woman who appeared adept at presiding over the business at hand. Her dark hair trimmed to an attractive length. Her average figure appeared agile and athletic.

The clerk read the charges against the three, Murders, drug dealing worldwide..."

Judge Lioness' interrupted saying, "Thank you it's too long to read it... we'll deal with all the charges ... documentation... they're too numerous we'll do them one by one, I'll deviate from protocol this once... everyone has copies of the charges..."

The clerk answers, "Yes Your Honor thank you."

Judge Lioness crashed her gavel down, saying, "Mr. Prosecutor I understand one prisoner want to testify in his own behalf...proceed Mr. Prosecutor call him to the stand."

The Prosecutor said, "We call Mr. Biggars to the stand."

Biggars is escorted to the stand...took the oath..."To tell the truth and nothing but the truth...so help me."

Suddenly he was holding a sleeve gun in his hand, with the other arm holding the clerk around the shoulder ... the gun discharged and the bullet strikes the judges clerk in his thigh he collapses with blood pooling on the floor ... the audience screams... and try to take cover...Biggars held the clerk that administered the oath, saying , "Judge...I'm getting out of here ....or she will no longer breath air on this earth." he drags the clerk toward the nearest exit...the audience crying out in terror as he goes by... aiming the gun to cover the spectators.

Guards try to get close enough to take him down, and free the clerk.

Biggars passes close to the three women... who simultaneously attacked...

Bertha karate chops him on either side of his throat...

Martha disabled the hand around the clerks shoulder...

Ida twisted the gun out of his hand all done swiftly...not giving Biggars time to act.

Biggars falls to the floor sobbing, "Just kill me...the bitch killed my dog. I'm ruined everything I've worked for is gone."

The Judge said, "...Get him out of here...We'll be in recess until ten o'clock tomorrow morning." She crashes her gavel down and left the bench.

Newsmen ran from the court room and those with smart phones hurriedly report their stories.

Biggars is lead from the court room...a broken old man.

The court room scene was broadcast over all news channels.

TELEVISION and RADIO NEWROOMS... across the nations filled living rooms everywhere with the court room happening of the day.

Judge Lioness, said "I thank you all for allocution for your sins...saves the county treasury for over twenty years. Now that said....I am speaking to the duly appointed Police Commissioner... by Mayors who trusted you over the years. You have really given your office a black eye...
And you Ms. Dunbar...a really knowledgeable woman who could be helping mankind...you chose to line your pockets with ill gotten gains...
To the three of you... computer programmers have recovered three billions. Nine hundred million dollars you all accumulated and stored over the years... along with the tons of drugs you attempted to scatter over the world... since you wanted the drugs so much...we want you to see what's been done... first it was weighed.... Watch this little film we devised just for you."
On the screen in a closed area the enormous mound of drugs was blown up and burned.
Biggars cried out in agony shaking his head...and the money was disbursed for the poor with the masses, He crumpled, saying "All my money gone in seconds." the shock was too much. He laps' into a deep depression.
The Police Commissioner, Biggars was lucid enough and Dunbar all threw themselves on the mercy of the court...
Those with lesser crimes turned on their employers for lesser sentences ...giving... States evidence.

Judge Lioness said, "It is my duty to write the sentences...the three Of you are sentenced to three hundred years and a day equally... without a chance of parole... for murders, attempted murder of unborn twins, narcotic and the list goes on. This court is adjourned."
She slammed her gavel down and left the bench.

This is K.I.S.G... with 'Up To Date News ...Lisa Harmon reporting we bring you the DeHaven twins...
Phillip and Peter two handsome young men casually dressed to the nines... accompanied by IDA, Martha and Bertha they amble out to a stand up ovation... uproarious applause and whistle...they shake hands with Lisa... and seated.
Lisa said, "We have so much to report today...let's get right to it... You have had a tumultuous life ...can you tell us anything about that?"
Phillip answered, "It started over twenty years ago....My mother was Caroline DeHaven ...she was pregnant with Peter and me."

Peter continues, "She was assaulted by a cowardly act...her killer crept upon her and bludgeoned her by striking her on her pregnant abdomen causing her to to need the doctor to work feverishly to save her life and us...but ended by saving Phillip and me... mom did see us before she expired."

Phillip added, "Our dad was Carter DeHaven he was gunned down in his driveway weeks later, another cowardly act of murder."

Lisa asked, "Were these killings ever solved?"

Peter answers ,"No...there were two people found in what was claimed to be a stolen car from SELLERS CONGLOMERATE...no one was found... all had alibis." Phillip replied.

Phillip adds, "Needless to say there was lots of money to shield their crookedness ...The stolen company car burned so hot until the teeth were not useable. There was no D.N.A., all when everybody was out of town or otherwise occupied...total dead end."

Lisa said. "You had no chance to plead for your life?"

Peter said, "I don't think we were considered to be human... you know... not seen meant we didn't exist."

Lisa continues "I understand friends separated you allowing you to grow up safe...and here you are...I understand you're both getting married soon."

"Yes a happy occasion for a change... we need the rest." Peter said smiling.

Lisa smiling said, "It's late in coming, but never too late to enjoy. K.I.S.G., thanks you for giving us your time. Phillip and Peter ...

We have enough time to speak to some of your saviors...Ida, Martha and Bertha please come up here we must hear from you."

They came forward from the front row....to loud applause to be seated.

Lisa said, "Welcome to, 'UP TO DATE NEWS' We have very little time... I'll ask you Ida...what do you think of the final sentence...?"

Ida chuckled saying."Biggars is so contrary ...he might live those three hundred and more to spite us...especially without Boregard his dog."

Laughter.

"Bertha what did you say about the Police Commissioner?" Lisa asked.

"I said he was P.C., for all those years...and as slippery as okra." Bertha replied.

Lisa said, "That is a rather slippery answer yum... when Biggars threatened the clerk... how did you feel about the way you all took him down, very brave of you."

Martha said, "Not bravery...You didn't ask why... Biggars threatened our adopted children repeatedly and we let him know we aren't taking that from him ever again... he got the point"

"I agree." Lisa responded.

Ida asked' "Can I say something about us?"

Lisa replied. "Sure."

Ida said, "We might be aged...I must tell you we have seen it all...we have heard it all... and we have done it all... We just can't remember it all... but family is everything forever." She bowed... Laughter and applause.

Lisa said, "After that...we thank our guests for coming ...till we meet again for 'UP TO DATE NEWS'."

WEEK LATER:

The wedding chapel on the DeHaven estate...is filled with friends, relatives and the newly adopted three grandmothers, Ida, Martha and Bertha...the three were obligated to cry during the ceremony.

The brides were dressed in cleverly designed white gowns...that covered their baby bumps.

The reverend Doctor HAYES instructed, "Take your brides hand in yours... We are gathered here to join these men and women in holy matrimony... to have and to hold until death do you part..."

Soft music swells in the background:

The grandmas cried audibly...

The Minister ended with ..."I now pronounce you man and wife ...you may kiss your brides."

The throwing of rice and flowers ... then to the waiting carriages... with the fringe on top...They were off to DeHaven Manor for change of clothes, the banquet... singing and dancing.

Banquet in the great hall of DeHaven Manor.

The tables were splendidly decorated with upscale China dinner ware... crystal and linen table clothes...

Both couples dance their first dance together as man and wife... to romantic music.

Phillip felt a thump in the solar plexus, and said. "How did you do that?"

Leyla asked, "Do what?"

Phillip said, "Punch me in the stomach."

Leyla answers laughing, "Oh that ... the babies does that all the time... they just kicked....I felt it... I didn't know you felt it, too."

Phillip stopped dancing, saying, "And ...are you keeping something from me? ...Angel Face ...You said they."

"Honey I am sorry... I just found out when Kassi and ... I... Angel face had our check up with the doctor...we are both having twins." Leyla said in a matter of fact tone of voice.

Phillip said to Peter dancing nearby. "Peter… Did you know we're having twins!?"

Peter yelled, "What!?… Kassi, sweetheart we have to talk more…you never said we were having twins!" He picked her up, saying loudly, "Hey everybody we're having twins!"

There was happy applause, kisses, slaps on the backs…singing of Charley Prides song …'Kiss and Angel good morning etc'… the banquette turns into the happy occasion of the year.

Phillip looked around at the dancers then to Leyla saying. "Should you be dancing …you should stop, sit down… are you sure you can do fast movements in your condition?"

Leyla answered, "Honey it's not a condition … I am pregnant….young and healthy… I'll sit after we do the Tango together … I promise."

The Tango went smoothly… done by Leyla and Phillip… Kassi and Peter both couples on the dance floor.

There is dancing for … all to the brides and grooms favorite…then the crowds music was free for all…anything goes. Mexican hat dance… Mambo, Salsa, Twist, music became a Boogie Woogie by Ida…. Wild happy music… and finally a Conga line.

Wedding and Banquette over…both brides lie curled up in their beds asleep…both grooms looked at them proudly.

The law Offices of District Attorney… JAMES GARRETT… he welcomed the defense attorney JACK DANIELS, saying, "I'm glad you could come so soon…make yourself comfortable…can I offer you a drink or water anything you want."

Both attorneys are dressed elegantly… by Brooks Brothers…of New York… one in charcoal gray…the other dark blue suit… Their dress was up to the code for any well paid attorney…

James Garrett D.A, said, "We have inherited the most problematic case in history… The after math of the forfeiture of all that accumulated ill gotten gains… the three made. not a win…win situation… "

Jack Daniels responded, "The workers were there for salaries to care for their families…they're all jumping ship, we have confessions, writs, affidavits', photos of the operations, Xerox copies…they had a damn competent record keeper. "

Garrett answered," the money was well documented… how much and where it went… the three planners goose is cooked."

Jack Daniels responded, "I agree…"

James said, "These bad boys and woman have been active for at least twenty years… we caught a lucky break… two kids OTTO and OMAR very smart … found a method for reclaiming the billions…of accumulated… money …they have shown our department how they have found over three billion and nine hundred millions so far."

Jack answered, "I heard about the little people who were instrumental in the discovery of bales of …records, papers and files… the records were kept meticulously."

James said, "Not to mention the cold blood murder of a pregnant mother and her husband… the attempted killing of unborn twins…" he paused momentarily, then said, "I suggested they throw themselves on the mercy of the court… they took my suggestion."

Jack said, "I'll get back to you." he stood, extended his hand and left the office.

This is K.I.S.G., Lisa Harmon reporting 'Up To Date News'…This just in…the two men and woman in the trial of the century…has been put on suicide watch…Mr. Biggars …is in and out of an ongoing depression…He cries out for Boregard his dead dog at times …. And whispers constantly…. The former big man on the block has cracked."

"The Police Commissioner…does not speak of his involvement that helped his co-conspirators, he yells at times, 'Let me out of here… 'I am the police Commissioner'… he threatens. 'You will all be sorry…' he couldn't wrap his mind around the fact that he was caught after twenty plus years … he's being kept in solitaire confinement as all three are on suicide watch… Dunbar the planner is a brilliant woman …who could have been a help to mankind…to bad she moved to the dark side… that's the way it is for some people and greed… that's it for today I'm … Lois Harman saying …'This Is 'Up to Date News' until tomorrow."

Ida, Martha and Bertha, in a department store baby wears section, Ida said, "I'll get the furniture."

Martha asked, "" Why you?"

Ida answers, "You have better taste in clothes…you'll have a chance to criticize, okay."

Bertha said, "She got you there."

Martha saying, "You're right…let's get started… we'll meet at the cash register in an hour with our selections."

Hours later Hanes Department Store delivered … a truck loaded with baby supplies.

Bertha said, "There are no diapers…I ordered Egyptian cotton and I am having them made."

Ida asked, "Why cotton from Egypt…? Kids don't care about where the diapers are made as long as they have something to catch the pee or whatever, comes out naturally."

Martha said, "She's right the cotton is the best for our grand children's little bottoms... the kids will love it, too."

Ida said sarcastic, "Yeah...right."

The adopted grandmothers were busy giving instructions on where everything goes in the common room of DeHaven Manor... they would have an object moved ...then change their minds... all would have the workers move the room around until they were exhausted.

The newlywed couples entered the common room to find a complete nursery, beds, bath tables, and closets, four of everything complete.

Surprised, Phillip said," We have been invaded by the baby decorators... and here they are."

As the three proud grandmas entered the room.

Bertha asked, "Well... do you like it?"

Peter answered, "Yes overwhelmed is the word ...but you shouldn't have done all this yourself."

Ida replied, "I am sorry the diapers didn't arrive from Egypt...not to worry they'll be here on the next plane."

Kassi and Leyla gasped saying, "From Egypt?" she and Leyla were looking at the furniture everything arranged and practical.

Phillip responded, "Why Egypt?"

Martha answered, "Grandma Ida is having the diapers made there with the best cotton on the planet...she heard that somewhere."

Ida proud of her purchase said, "Nothing is too good for our babies little bottoms...do I get a man?"

Kassi asked, "What's left for us to buy?"

Martha saying, "You can get the baby clothes... you know about colors and ...I'm not into baby clothes... beside you are doing your part... how is that coming?"

Leyla responded, "Still kicking... as a matter of fact they are kicking right now."

Grandmas rush to feel, Peter and Phillip could only stand by and watch asked, "What about us we had a role to play in the whole thing." Ida said, "Not to worry we'll get to you in good time." laughing.

The mutual happiness is contagious.

MONTHS LATER:

Two bedrooms occupants are sound asleep, "Leyla suddenly awoke feeling warm fluid oozing into her bed, and she said, "Phillip I think my water just broke..."

Phillip sits up sleepy, saying, "...Are you sure...it could be just sweat," he rolled over trying to fall asleep...He felt the wet sheet, said "Great!!! It's all wet!"

Leyla said, "Who gives a damn... you did this to me... I saved that part for you...now you're all wet..." another pain. "Ooooooh this is not going to

be easy and it hurts like crazy… I'm having another pain here it comes I"
Phillip said, "You're having the babies … now?!!!"

Leyla flabbergasted. "Of course Phillip… what the hell do you think I am doing at this hour, with a wet bed and the stomach ache of the damn century…It hurts… you asked me if I'm having the baby… you missed counted… hell no I'm having two babies understand ! !!"

The telephone rang…Phillip answered, "Yes Peter it just happened Leylas just broke, she's a bit testy using language I haven't heard from her…it's not suppose to happen now at this hour… we're supposed to be at the Laire snug in a dry bed…they're early.'

Peter said, "Kassi is too cool… where are the overnight bags?"

Kassi said, "Whose cool…we sent the bags last week… this is going to be a damn rough night… I just called for the car and the grandmas… they're on the way to the Laire …Peter we have to get dressed."

Leyla bent over with pain, Phillip hurriedly continues. "She just had a pain… I gotta go… you called for the van."

Peter said, "Meet us at the van."

Kassi started to say again," I sent the bags…pooch." as a severe cramp caused her to cry out… "We need to hurry the Doctor said both of us will have a c-section…we gotta hurry….it could mean death for one or both of us and the babies. It happens in multiple births."

Phillip feverishly searched through the neat closets, dropping clothes on hangers to the floor. Asking, "Where are my pants, and shirts they do not seem to be here.'

Peters demeanor changed saying, "Phillip the cramps are getting closer together… we should get started… forget the clothes call the police for an escort NOW…" he turned to Kassi, saying,"

"I'm so sorry about your pain… I wish I could help bare it."

Kassi answered, "We had the mutual desire for this pain and I'd do it again…but we need to get through this…first."

Peter asked, "Should I carry you…would that help?"

Kassi smiling said, "No…but it would work for me… just help me, keep me standing…we'll make it."

He answers, "That's my baby… we'll make it." He supported her as they slowly walked….Kassi had to stop momentarily bending over for a pain to pass.

Kassi relaxes, said, "That one's passed for now… let's hurry…we have ten miles to go… I can't endure too many cramps like that…I am feeling the pressure, the babies have turned into the birth canal …call Dr. Morton tell him the babies have turned, he should get ready for an emergency delivery."

After the wild ride and bumps in the streets… with police sirens screaming through the night… they arrived at the Laire.

Shaken they were met at the emergency entrance… nurses and Doctor Morton waiting with stretchers, other personnel whisked the patients inside.

Phillip and Peter were nervous and completely, disheveled hair unbrushed … half dressed in damp pajamas… t-shirts and slippers without socks.

Dr. Morton said, "Fathers…follow the nurses into the wash room… When you're changed into scrubs. hurry Kassi will not wait much ;longer."

Peter asked, "Where are you taking my wife?"

Dr. Morton answers, "To the delivery room… now go with the nurses they'll get you situated, I have this covered… now go and hurry. "as they turn to the grandmas.

In the Laire the nurses and grandmas took over, the dads were taken to wash their hands and to change into scrubs.

"Why can't we go with them now… she's in agony? " Phillip worried asked.

Ida answers, " You will… after you've cleaned up…look at you all messy our babies are clean… now go with the nurse she'll help you change and then take you to the delivery room…now go, we got this…you have to hurry… our babies will not wait."

The daddies enter the delivery room scrubbed and gowned…looking anxiously around for their wives who were in stirrups, sedated…hospital equipment, oxygen hissed, sterile trays arranged neatly with other essentials…

Dads went to the moms held their hands. at a lost to know more to do.

Masked and gowned nurses and doctors were at their stations doing their jobs.

After the first screaming child was born… a procession of births… a nurse for each to take them to wash and the pediatrician to examine… Later to show the sleeping children to their parents in their assigned room…the adopted grandmas' ooooh and aaaaahed…everything was right with the world.

Kassi said, "Leyla and I've had a busy day …I think we're due a nap, we need the rest… dads would you like to sleep in these over sized hospital beds with us?" happily, glad to do something, they climbed under the sheets cradled the moms in their arms...

Soon all were sleeping.

Grandmas tipped toed in and out as proud as punch... visited the viewing room window to see the babies again. Snickering as they went along... planning...passing nurses and other hospital employees as they went about their grandmotherly work.

The couples sit on the solarium of the Laire overlooking the mountain greenery in the distance.

Leyla asked, "How do you feel about our naming our babies?"

Phillip responded, "Does that mean you two have suggestions?"

Kassi answers, "Yes we have discussed names...we wanted to run it by you before we decided."

Leyla nods.

Peter said smiling, "Kassi ...You silver tongued devil how can we refuse... okay run it by us."

Leyla said, "I like our son to be 'Michael DeHaven'...and 'Michelle DeHaven' our little girl."

Kassi laughing replied, "I thought of our son as 'Skylar DeHaven' and 'Scarlet DeHaven' our daughter, after all you are fifty percent responsible... what do you think?"

Peter said, "I think you have a winner...I like it sweetheart." He kissed her.

Phillip said, "'Angel Face' ...You both put thought into your decision... and we love that you included us fifty percent and all."

Nurses brought the two sets of twins out for the parents to feed their children...and get use to their names.

Each parent took a child in their arms... nurses taught them how to hold the children and give them the bottles to feed and burp.

TWELVE MONTHS LATER:

There is an oversized padded playpen...built for both families filled with toys of all kinds...radios... records... books all in each Childs cubicles. Everything old and modern a child would examine... enjoy... dads and moms are able to sit with their children and watch them grow...play and learn to crawl.... Walking falling down and getting up to do it again...

Nurses are on duty to care for the children personal needs...see that they're cared for....

Grandmothers.... Bought a carriage to take their grand children for rides around the now two estates....

Sellers conglomerate was forfeit due to their crimes...

The grandmothers were busy designing cases for the children...and books to stock them, musical instruments.... Songs to sing....parents to dance and sing with....Children had teachers to show them how to play the instruments.

Dads watched their children and enjoyed the growing up time they had missed… how they interact with other people… even the poopy diapers…burping up formula…messy eating…falls…learning to talk.
Love grows in the family especially the moms and dads.

K.I.S.G… News studios…with Edgar Killgallen….news commentator…
He says…"We have exclusive news just in…The three infamous collaborators in crime has forfeit any claims to the their fortunes real and other wise… the accumulated wealth… due to their crimes against country and society… the known murders…. robbing two unborn children now twenty plus years later. Namely the human robbery of a life with a family. The accumulated wealth over twenty plus years is estimated at present to be close to three trillion to date and counting… The I.R.S., is calculating, that owed to the United States Treasury….and the count continues….Ladies and Gentlemen we will update the news as it arise. This is Edgar Killgallan saying until tomorrow."

The grandmas has outfitted the children's playroom with each having shelving for books, radios, disc player , instruments Drum sets, key boards…all teaching the children to play all the toys imaginable…enjoying the task as much as the children…Watching as the kids inspected and tested everything eagerly.

Dads created bathrooms with double tubs for two.

Phillip said to Peter, "Best idea we ever had to date….I'll see you after the bath."
Peter replies, "Great idea… I'll show Kassi… I'm calling her right now." As he dials the phone. Saying when answered, "Hi sweetheart meet me in our den I have something to show you. Yes right now…you'll love it…"
Kassi asked, "Where are you calling from…?"
Peter replies, "From the den…where else? To Phillip… Peter said."See you later."

He arrives moments later, Kassi asked."What now …I'm not cooking today."
Peter said, "Close your eyes… it's a surprise…I'll guide you."
She walked arms extended. With him guiding her.
He said inside the bathroom, "Open your eyes."
She did as instructed, squealed with delight, "Oh my goodness, I'm taking a bath now," and starts to take her clothes off, she asked , "I assumed this is for the two of us… want you join me," they both are in

the over sized tub together…soaping each other, splashing …enjoying the bath.

Peter asked, "Don't you like it?"

"Who wouldn't I love it." said Kassi laughing happily soaping herself and him.

Peter replied, "Bring your soft, soapy, slippery body over here."

She glides into his arms… sings to him "SMOKE GETS IN YOUR EYES."

Four children reach their fifth birthday… there is a birthday party for the twins… children from the colony are there as guests for lunch… the party begins… children dance some in place….other moves smoothly around the floor…clap their hands…

There is a cacophony of sounds CHILDREN AND GRANDMAS PLAY, ALL INSTRUMENTS they watched the children as they examined, played everything.

The four DeHaven children show improvement in playing the instruments… their parents are proud.

Two grandmas played the key boards showing the kids what to do, they all sang children songs… there was story time and last but not least the drums. The party was enjoyed by all.

Phillip asked Peter laughing, "Do you or I hide the drums… Ida bought two sets and a base."

Peter responded, "Another thing we can do together… I'm with you anytime… don't forget the base."

Leyla sings "THIS CAN'T BE LOVE…because I feel so well." she and Phillip go to their quarters.

Children fight falling asleep before the song is finished… children from the colony are taken home.

Twins are tucked in… by the nannies.

Kassi ends with a song to Peter "I WANT A SUNDAY KIND OF LOVE" as they walk to their quarters and close the door.

THE END

Story by: Imogene Grant
@imogenegrant3

www.ingramcontent.com/pod-product-compliance
Lightning Source LLC
Chambersburg PA
CBHW040547170726
48295CB00012B/617